THIRTEEN GHOSTLY ENCOUNTERS AT WIRSING MANOR

Sindy Smith

PublishAmerica
Baltimore

© 2012 by Sindy Smith.
All rights reserved. No part of this book may be reproduced, stored in a retrieval system or transmitted in any form or by any means without the prior written permission of the publishers, except by a reviewer who may quote brief passages in a review to be printed in a newspaper, magazine or journal.

First printing

All characters in this book are fictitious, and any resemblance to real persons, living or dead, is coincidental.

PublishAmerica has allowed this work to remain exactly as the author intended, verbatim, without editorial input.

Hardcover 9781462667369
PUBLISHED BY PUBLISHAMERICA, LLLP
www.publishamerica.com
Baltimore

Printed in the United States of America

To the ghosts of Wirsing Manor.

Some of us believe in ghosts without ever having lived with them. Some of us believe in ghosts because we want to. We want to believe a part of us can continue on in this earthly realm, and still interact with the living. Then, there are those of us who believe in ghosts because we have lived with them, and know that they are real, that they are in fact something. But what that something is, called a ghost, continues to remain a mystery.

My family and I lived with ghosts, or whatever they were, for over a decade, and I know that I believe in whatever that something is. This something some of us calls ghosts, never harmed me or my family in the imposing fourteen room home we shared with them at 507 Mascoutah Avenue in Belleville, Illinois, but we definitely knew they were there.

When I first saw the ruin, which I came to call Wirsing Manor, I looked beneath the gloom, grime and cobwebs and saw the grand home it had once been.

It had been built in the 1840's by Henry Wirsing, a wealthy German immigrant, for himself and his bride, Margaretha Ehret. Henry Wirsing was the proprietor of the Flora Gardens Saloon and Recreation Center, next door to 507 Mascoutah Avenue, then known as the Mascoutah Plank Road. The Flora Gardens dance hall burned to the ground on Christmas Day, 1864, but Henry rebuilt it, and ran it for a number of years thereafter.

Margaretha Wirsing gave birth at the home to her five children. Louisa, the youngest daughter, never married and lived in the home until her death from consumption at the age of 31. Another child, George Wirsing is believed to have died there from a tragic accident while in his thirties. Mr. And Mrs. Wirsing died at the home in their 80's. All of the family members wakes were held at the family residence in the front parlor, and are documented in old newspapers at the Belleville Public Library. Rumor has it that during the Second World War, when the home was converted into a boarding house, that a double homicide occurred there, although, I was not able to confirm this. It is true though, that throughout the years, numerous people have died in the home.

Wirsing Manor was a wreck when I purchased it in 1994 with my late husband Edward Smith.

Wirsing Manor had all of the grand features that an old house lover dreamed of. It boasted fourteen large rooms, and three bath rooms. A lovely winding walnut staircase began in the foyer and lead to the second floor. To the left of the foyer was the front parlor, and through there, a large door to the left lead to the study, and off that, a bathroom with the original empire bathtub, a pedestal sink, and an antique toilet.

Through the front parlor was the formal dining room with the original fireplace mantel, (the fireplace opening had been bricked in over the years). Five inch heart pine floors were still intact, and large walnut double pocket doors lead into a new kitchen that was converted from a second parlor. Directly off the kitchen was the laundry room, which had been the original kitchen, and inside of one of the walls was a wall brick oven that was closed off. To the right of the kitchen, a doorway lead to the old brick sidewalk outside that went to the well pump.

Back inside, through the new kitchen, was a back hallway, which lead to the servant's stairway on one side, and to the library on the other. If you went straight through the library you would be end up back inside the front foyer.

Thankfully, over every door in the home were the transoms, which still held original 19th century glass panes.

Wirsing Manor would have been the perfect setting for the Nancy Drew stories. It was the most amazing place in which I have ever lived.

At the end of the winding staircase in the front foyer was a hallway with a landing, which was where I had my sitting room. To the right of the sitting room area was the master bedroom, and off that was the nursery, where my daughter Lindsay slept. Through a doorway off the nursery room was another bathroom with an antique claw foot tub and original pedestal basin. The door to the left opened into another large room, which had the original fireplace mantel. That bedroom was nearly as large as the master bedroom, and it went out into the back hallway. From the back hallway, you could get to the guest room, that had a step down bathroom off of it.

The back hallway lead to the servant's stairway, which lead down into the lower back hall and opened to the kitchen and back porch. There was a tiny drop down hallway that lead to the basement. The door to the basement was made from wooden planks, and had old strap hinges. There was an old wooden peg that went into an iron ring that held the door closed. Down in the basement, a similar door hung from old posts that opened into a small stairway that dropped down into a large brick wine cellar. The gentleman I purchased Wirsing Manor from, Mr. Lightfoot, told me the basement was once part of the underground railway. (How he came by that information, I do not know.) The wine cellar was huge, measuring 12 feet by 16 feet. The entire room was made from brick, and had an arched ceiling, brick floor, and iron hooks which hung from the ceiling (God only knows what they were used for!) The basement was creepy, to say the least, and I avoided it by pretending it wasn't there, going down only when I had to replace a fuse or do something essential for the workings of the house.

Upstairs on the second floor off the back hallway, was a door that went to an upstairs porch with a stairway that lead to the attic. The attic was another place that was odd and creepy to me. You had to go out onto that porch to get to the attic. There was no other way up. Once up the rickety stairway, there was a wooden hatch door, which had to be lifted and dropped against the outer wall. The attic was large enough to land a small plane in, and it was dark and dank, with wide plank flooring, and loaded with bats! Not baseball bats, but real live bats! When I lived there, there was a colony of 250 to 300 of the creepy creatures. They would get really excited and start flying around when someone would go into the attic. When they started flying, I would just freak out, and run down the rickety stairs, pulling the hatch door shut behind me. This was another part of the house that I avoided at all costs. It was just weird up there, certainly not my idea of a quiet retreat from the outside world.

The grounds around the home consisted of approximately an acre, containing old growth trees, and remnants of once proud flower beds and planting areas, a chicken coop, and the remains of a carriage house, where son Adam Wirsing, founded the Wirsing Carriage Works so many years ago.

So many pieces of the past were still intact that I could imagine myself back in time at this historical place. Wirsing Manor enchanted me, and I loved living there and thinking how it was when the Wirsing family lived there.

I believe the ghosts of the people that lived there and loved the place never left, or if they did, they somehow found a portal to return, from the world of the past, to the world of the present, and, perhaps, on into the world of the future.

I do know that if I had been one of the Wirsing family members that I would not have wanted to leave the place either. I truly don't think some of them ever did. I know that even though I sold the old place and moved on, part of me still exists there.

I wonder sometimes how we would ever know if we were ghosts going back to a place that we once loved. How would we know if we were just living there in the present, or were just going back to visit in time? How would we truly know? Think about it. And with that thought, I will leave you with thirteen of my favorite **true** ghost stories to share with you from my time at a really haunted house, known to me, as Wirsing Manor.

I.

Footsteps In The Parlor

    After an entire day and evening of sanding floors with an electric floor sander, Ed and I decided to sit in the front parlor on some old lawn chairs that we had brought with us (this room later became our formal living room). Ed and I were sitting there, the room dimly lit by just two lights, when first I, and then he, heard footsteps coming down the darkened foyer. At first I thought it was just I who heard what sounded like heavy soled shoes shuffling down the hallway outside of the parlor room. I said to Ed in a whisper, "Did you hear that?"

    He said, "Yes, I did. It's a ghost." My late husband was as straight as an arrow, and not given to belief in superstitions or the supernatural, but from the look on his face, I knew he was dead serious in his statement. Believe me, what we heard was real! It sounded like a large man with heavy soled shoes walking down the hallway. And it had stopped just as quickly as it had started. This was my first ghost experience, at Wirsing Manor, and it wouldn't be my last. It was only the first of many experiences that I was to encounter there at Wirsing Manor. Maybe it was Mr. Wirsing trying to figure out what Ed and I were doing to the floors.

II.

The Library Door Closes

One morning, about a week after I heard the footsteps, I was working in the foyer. I was on a ladder stripping one hundred year old wallpaper from the original plaster walls and was alone in the house. All of the doors to the house were locked, as they always were. I started thinking about the Wirsing family, and I decided to tell the Wirsings what I was going to do to their house. I said out loud, "I'm going to turn the house into a showplace, so don't worry about your home, I'm going to take good care of it, because I think I love it as much as you do."

A moment later, while still up on the ladder and pulling off a piece of the wallpaper, I saw the door between the foyer and library, which was fully open and against the wall, slowly begin to close. I just stood on the ladder in amazement and watched it. It was not as if a breeze or gust of wind had caught it and pushed or slammed it shut, or that maybe something had shaken the door and made it close. From the time I saw it begin to move, until the time the latch caught, and the door fully closed, more than a dozen seconds had elapsed. I slowly got down from the ladder, went over to the closed door, and stood for a moment just looking at it. I jumped and jumped, up and down, in front of the door trying to get it to move.

It did not rattle or move one bit. I slowly opened the door, and pushed it open, against the wall, as it had been. It stayed opened. I checked the front double doors in the foyer, and the doors and windows in adjacent rooms. All were closed. I did not feel any drafts. I went over to the door again and jumped up and down again on the foyer side of the door, which opened into the library to see if I could get it to close. It didn't budge, not even a little. Nothing happened like this with the door between the foyer and the library again that day, or any other day while I lived there. Why did the door close? Could it have been one of the Wirsings?

III.

Groaning In The Bedroom

    I was really excited to finally get to spend my first night in Wirsing Manor after Ed and I had worked so hard on it for months. We had finally sold our other home, and had moved all of our furniture and things into our new old home. We were really tired, but so happy to have all of our things in one place. The last thing that we did before calling it a day was to put together our four poster cherry wood bed. I lit some oil lamps, put on the bed linens and crawled into bed. I laid there watching the shadows dance on the walls. Ed had fallen asleep. I was just starting to relax, and was admiring the room. It was very quiet, and then suddenly it started. It was some sort of noise like groaning, almost like someone groaning in pain.

    Ok, now I was starting to freak out! I woke Ed up, and asked him if he had heard anything. He said no, that I needed to go to sleep because I was overly tired. Then it started again. It was like someone was dying or something. I asked him if he heard it that time, and he said yes! I asked him what it was, and he said it must be the ghost. All I could do was pull the covers over my head and hope that whatever it was wouldn't find a way to crawl in bed with me or hurt me. Then it stopped. After that night, it never happened again. Did Henry want to scare us?

IV.

Did Someone Break Into The House?

    The next night, I was a little bit afraid to go to sleep. I mean, after all of that groaning the night before wouldn't you be? But restoring an old house will make you tired, so upstairs I went. Ed came to bed a little later. We started to drift off to sleep, and then it started. It sounded like someone was downstairs moving the furniture around, or knocking things over. Then, I heard some sort of music from yesteryear. I thought someone had broken into the house. I also thought maybe I was going crazy. *Why would a burglar break into my house and start playing music,* was what I was thinking. That would definitely have been one weird burglar. I told Ed to go downstairs and check it out. He took our old baseball bat with him and headed downstairs. I waited outside the bedroom door with the new baseball bat. The noises suddenly stopped. I could hear Ed walking all around downstairs checking the windows and doors. He came back upstairs, and said everything seemed fine. He said, "Sindy, it is the ghost. You just have to accept the fact that there are ghosts in this house."

    "How does someone accept that, Ed?" I said to him. He just rolled over and said goodnight. Then the noises started again. And once again, I pulled the covers over my head, and got as close to Ed as I could. This sort of activity happened at least a half a dozen times after we moved in.

I always thought that someone must have broken in when I heard it, but Ed just reassured me that it was the ghost! How reassuring is that?

V.

The Smell Of Sauerkraut And Pipe Tobacco

Often, while being in the house, Ed and I would smell sauerkraut cooking. We thought this was really weird, because we never cooked sauerkraut. I did have some in a can, but I never made it, because I always thought it smelled terrible. Who knows, maybe we were smelling some memory that the house had of sauerkraut being cooked on a stove by the Wirsings, who happened to be German. From what I hear, Germans like sauerkraut, so maybe they cooked a lot of it in the house. I'm Italian, and cooked a lot of pasta dishes there, but no one ever told me they smelled linguine with red clam sauce. However, many of our friends smelled sauerkraut cooking.

The other thing that we smelled many times was the aroma of pipe tobacco drifting through the rooms. Neither of us smoked, so we thought this was really strange. I always thought that whoever, or whatever was smoking had very good taste, because the stuff smelled great. Sometimes I would smell it when I was outside. It was as if someone was following me around while smoking a pipe. Maybe Mr. Wirsing liked to smoke.

VI.

Up And Down The Servant's Stairway

    One Sunday afternoon while Ed was barbecuing on the side porch, I was making potato salad inside. While Ed was flipping the burgers, I heard it. Footsteps were going up the servant's stairway in the back part of the house, which was just off of the kitchen. I asked Ed to come inside and listen. He sat down at the island, and listened. The footsteps started again, but this time they sounded like they were going down the staircase. Ed heard it, and gave his usual response. "Sindy, it's the ghost."

    Great, this place is crawling with ghosts. They smoke, cook, moan, close doors, walk around, move furniture, and play music, I thought. By this time I was starting to feel like I had a bunch of invisible roommates. Only they didn't pay any rent. It would have been great if they had!

VII.

Ed Meets Louisa, While Sindy Sleeps

    I love to sleep in on the weekends. (Don't we all?) It was a Saturday morning and I thought I would skip the early morning restoration work, so I stayed in bed. Ed knew that I liked to sleep in on Saturdays, so I thought it was odd that he had come into the bedroom and moved my arm and said, "Sindy, what were you doing going down the stairway so early? Did you go back up the front stairway? I didn't see you leave." *What in the world are you talking about, Ed?* I thought. He then told me he saw a woman out of the corner of his eye while he was making breakfast. She was in a long white night gown, which is what I wore to sleep in. He said she came down the servant's stairway, and went through the library. He assumed it was me, sleepwalking or roaming around early. There wasn't anyone else in the house, only the two of us. He told me that he thought it was Louisa Wirsing making a guest appearance. We both seemed freaked out by this episode. However, I never saw her. Maybe it was Louisa Wirsing, because she was born there, lived there her entire life and died there an old maid. Why she showed up that morning, who knows. Maybe she was after Edward!

VIII.

The Plumber Asked For a Box, And He Got One

I had to have a plumber come out to connect a gas line in our new kitchen. The plumber got there around 2:00 p.m. This guy was a tall, hefty, middle-aged man. He seemed to be a no nonsense kind of guy. He went outside to smoke about every half hour. Luckily for me, I didn't pay him by the hour.

While he was working on plumbing, I was painting. As dinner time approached, he was still working. I needed to make dinner for Ed, and making a meal was difficult because we hadn't rewired the house yet, and we only had two circuits for the entire house. I heard Ed come in, and a few minutes later I blew a fuse while using the microwave and the electric skillet at the same time. Now it was pitch black inside the house, and we heard screams coming from the basement where the plumber was working. Ed grabbed the flashlight and we headed down into the creepy basement. The plumber was freaking out.

Remember that this was a no nonsense kind of guy. When we got to him, he was shaking, sweating, and as white as, well, as a ghost, no pun intended. He told us that he needed a cardboard box to use for something, which he said out loud while talking to himself. Just as he did, a cardboard box from the other side of the basement floated through the air to him. That's when he started screaming.

I was speechless, and for once, so was Ed. Really, for this one I don't think Ed knew what to think. Things were just getting crazier and crazier. I said to the plumber, "Wow, you just had a close encounter of the third kind!" The plumber said, "Look lady, I don't care what kind of encounter I had, I just want to get my connection made and get the hell out of here." He made the final connection in record time and left. Ed told me he hoped the plumber did the job right, because there was no way we would ever get the guy to come back to our house. Perhaps George liked to play with boxes.

IX.

Someone, Or Something Watches Sindy

I always had the strange feeling that someone, or something was watching me in the bathroom, especially when I was taking a shower in the old claw foot bathtub with the wrap around shower curtain. This feeling became so overwhelming at times I had to open the shower curtain and look out just to make sure no one was in there with me. Of course, I knew rationally that there was no one in the bathroom with me, but it was really a strange feeling to think some ghost was watching me in the shower. Even if I had known the ghost, it still would have seemed strange. Maybe there was just a dirty little ghost in the house!

X.

Sindy Angers The Wirsings

Let's face it, restoring a fourteen room, 19th century house isn't cheap. It seemed as if Ed and I were in way over our heads financially, because this place was a real money pit. The movie by that name fitted us to a tee. Every time we had to fix something, we found four other things that were broken. So to fix the one thing that was broken meant you had to first fix the other things that were behind it that were broken too. Our bank account was dwindling, and our construction loan was being depleted rapidly.

One evening, Ed was sitting in the family room upstairs, and I just got fed up throwing money into the walls. So I yelled to Ed, "If the Wirsing family loves this house so much, then why can't they help me find some hidden gold coins, or some money under the floor boards, so we can get this hell-hole fixed!"

With that, the door that led to the back hallway and servant's stairway began to shake violently like someone was behind it, shaking the handle as hard as they could, to get our attention. They got our attention, all right. It was like someone or something was really upset with what I had said. Ed looked at me with big eyes, and suggested I never speak badly of the Wirsing family again. And guess what? I never did.

XI.

Who Are Those People Watching the Baby?

Several years had passed from the time we had begun our massive restoration of Wirsing Manor. Sometime in between painting, sanding, ripping out walls and adding walls, we had found a little time to bring our daughter into the world. Believe me, this was no easy task. I was hanging wallpaper while I was 37, and eight months pregnant. Really, what was I thinking? But then one May day, a lovely new life made her way into our hearts and home. Being the overprotective fanatic that I am, I had to have the crib right by my bed at all times. One evening I was completely exhausted, so I decided to put the baby in her crib and go to bed early. I next remember trying to wake up; I had my eyes open, and could see, but I was not able to move, because I was still not fully awake. I could see a man and a woman dressed in old fashioned clothing watching the baby in her crib. They just stood there, watching her. I quickly grabbed the baby, and they suddenly disappeared. I knew I was not dreaming. I never saw them again, but a friend of mine was in the formal living room one evening, and asked me if I could see the couple dressed in vintage clothing, standing in the corner! Could the couple have been Mr. And Mrs. Wirsing?

XII.

Holly Is Touched

My oldest daughter had moved back home for a while, and we let her have the guest room. Holly told me that the house *creeped* her out. She said she felt like someone was watching her all the time. She had the same kind of experience in the bathroom as I did. She never wanted to be alone in the house.

One day, Holly told me she had driven up the private drive in the back and saw me standing at the back door window, behind the lace curtain. Then, she said, when she got closer to the door, she realized that the face in the door was not mine. As she got closer, the face disappeared! I was upstairs at the other end of the house at the time. Holly started knocking on the door and ringing the door bell when she realized that it was not me she had seen. She told me she had gotten really scared that someone had broken in the house while I was in there. I told her I was upstairs, but nowhere near the back door.

Another time, Holly came screaming upstairs, and told me that while she was in the laundry room, something touched her face. I was thinking it was that dirty little ghost again.

XIII.

Who's Behind The Door?

One day I went shopping with my youngest daughter. By this time, there was an alarm system installed in the house. We did this, because as Holly said, the house was so large that if someone broke in downstairs we would never have heard them until it was too late. Ed and I thought she was probably right, so the alarm system made sense.

After a few hours out with a two year old, I had to get back home and take a nap. I was pushing forty now, and my stamina was diminishing. Gone was the thirty-four-year old who could go and go, and restore and restore all day.

I went upstairs and still had my two-year old in my arms. I was standing about six feet from the bathroom door, when suddenly the bathroom door handle started turning back and forth by itself. It was like someone was on the other side turning it repeatedly. I thought maybe someone had broken into the house, because I didn't set the alarm when I left that day.

I just stood there holding my young daughter thinking, *Oh my God*. I was sure someone was behind the door. I didn't know what to do, so I stood still, watching the door knob move back and forth. Then I thought, *Okay, just go open the door, and see what is going on. If someone is behind the door, they are not trying to come out.* So, bravely, I walked over to the door, turned the handle, and opened the bathroom door. There was nothing behind it. Nothing at all. Could it have been Adam Wirsing?

I hope you enjoyed these short ghost stories from my experiences living at Wirsing Manor. Maybe, someday, I will write about the rest of them.

THE END

Would you like to see your manuscript become a book?

If you are interested in becoming a PublishAmerica author, please submit your manuscript for possible publication to us at:

acquisitions@publishamerica.com

You may also mail in your manuscript to:

**PublishAmerica
PO Box 151
Frederick, MD 21705**

We also offer free graphics for Children's Picture Books!

www.publishamerica.com

PublishAmerica